Enid Blyton's

Night-time
TALES

For further information on Enid Blyton please contact www.blyton.com

ISBN 1-84135-031-1

Text copyright © The Enid Blyton Company
Design and illustration copyright © 1994 The Templar Company plc
Enid Blyton's signature is a trademark of The Enid Blyton Company

First published 2000
Second impression 2001

Published by Award Publications Limited,
1st Floor, 27 Longford Street, London NW1 3DZ

Printed in Singapore

Enid Blyton's

Night-time
TALES

AWARD PUBLICATIONS LIMITED

The Stories

1

The Toys'
New Palace

Illustrated by Pamela Venus

Jack and Tilly had built a palace with their bricks. It was a very good one – very tall and grand, with windows and a door and lots of towers and turrets. The children were pleased with it.

"It's a pity nobody ever lives in the houses and palaces we build," said Tilly. "They are just wasted, really. We build them, and then we knock them down."

"I wish we didn't have to knock *this* palace down," said Jack, looking at it proudly. "It really is one of the best we've ever made, don't you think? Look, Mummy! Don't you think our palace is good?"

"Splendid!" said Mummy. "But now it's time for bed so you must put your bricks away."

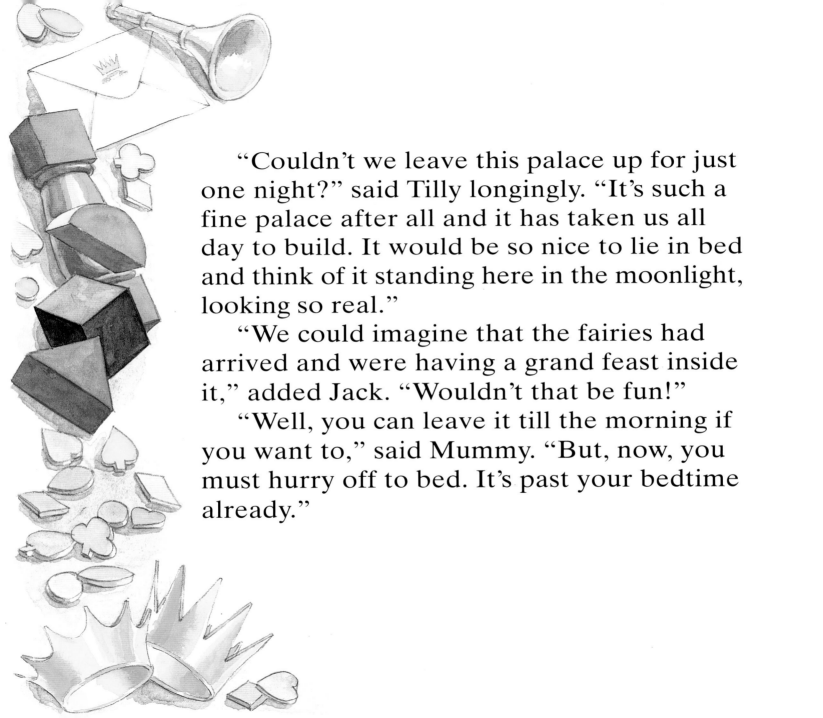

"Couldn't we leave this palace up for just one night?" said Tilly longingly. "It's such a fine palace after all and it has taken us all day to build. It would be so nice to lie in bed and think of it standing here in the moonlight, looking so real."

"We could imagine that the fairies had arrived and were having a grand feast inside it," added Jack. "Wouldn't that be fun!"

"Well, you can leave it till the morning if you want to," said Mummy. "But, now, you must hurry off to bed. It's past your bedtime already."

Little did the children realise that, as soon as they had left the room, their toys all started to come to life. The big teddy bear let all the toys out of the toy cupboard. The dolls woke up inside the doll's house. All the animals on the toy farm came awake and the clockwork train started running about all over the floor.

It happened every night and this night the toys were pleased to find that the children had left them a splendid palace to play in. They thought it was a very fine present indeed!

When the children were safely in bed, and the nursery was in darkness except for the big silver moon shining through the window, the big teddy bear ran right across the nursery floor and looked through the doorway of the fine wooden palace.

"I say! It's the best thing that ever was!" he called. "Come on toys! Look what the children have built for us! See this window – and that one – and look at the turrets and spires at the top. My, haven't they built it well!"

"It's splendid," said one of the dolls' house dolls. "Can we go inside?"

Just then there came a loud banging noise from just above them. It was someone knocking on the nursery window.

"Come in!" called the teddy bear, surprised that anyone could come calling so late at night. And he was even more astonished when a large grey mouse appeared on the windowsill wearing a postman's cap on his head. He carried a letter in his hand and was busy looking all around the nursery for someone particular to deliver it to.

"Does the clockwork mouse live here?" he asked.

"Oh yes!" squeaked the little mouse in astonishment, and he ran over to the postman. "Here I am!"

"I have a letter for you from the King of Mice," said the postman in an important voice, handing it over.

Then
he turned
on his tail and
was gone again. The
toys heard him pattering
away along the garden path.
The clockwork mouse stared at his
letter in surprise. Then he tore it open.

"Oh!" he said excitedly.
"Oh! Listen to this – the
King and Queen of the
Mice are coming to
visit the nursery!

They are on their way to Mouseland, and they have decided to stay here for the night! They ask if they can be my guests! Oh, what an honour it is to be sure!"

The clockwork mouse was so excited that he ran up and down the nursery without stopping. Up and down and up and down he went, until his clockwork ran down and the teddy had to wind him up again.

"There is only one problem," said the mouse when he had calmed down. "The toy cupboard is all very well, but it would be so much nicer if I had a special place where the King and Queen could stay. I've only my old box for them to sleep in, and nothing at all to offer them to eat. Oh dear, I wish I could think of something better! What shall I do?

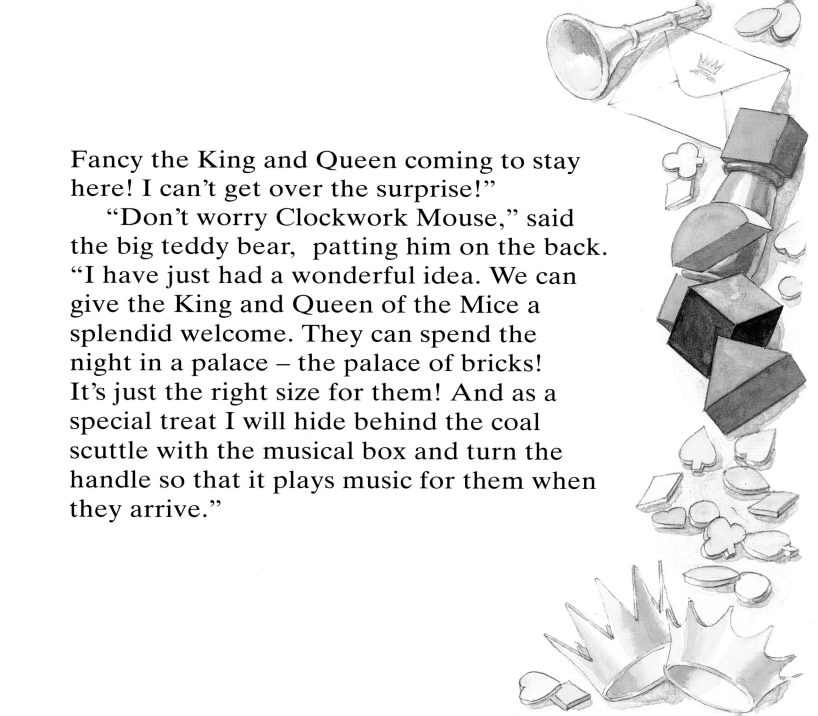

Fancy the King and Queen coming to stay here! I can't get over the surprise!"

"Don't worry Clockwork Mouse," said the big teddy bear, patting him on the back. "I have just had a wonderful idea. We can give the King and Queen of the Mice a splendid welcome. They can spend the night in a palace – the palace of bricks! It's just the right size for them! And as a special treat I will hide behind the coal scuttle with the musical box and turn the handle so that it plays music for them when they arrive."

"And I know where Jack dropped half his biscuit this morning," said the curly-haired doll excitedly. "It rolled into the corner of the floor over there!"

"And there are two sweets left in the toy sweet shop. I saw them there this afternoon!" said Panda. "Oh, Clockwork Mouse, you don't need to be worried – we will help you to welcome the King and Queen of the Mice. They are sure to have a lovely time!"

Well, you should have seen how those toys rushed about to get things ready!

First, they took all the furniture and the tiny rugs from the old dolls' house and put them into the palace of bricks. They found blankets and pillows for the tiny beds to make them comfortable. Then two of the rag dolls leaned out of the big nursery window and picked some flowers to put on the table.

The teddy bear found a little toy lantern and managed to hang it from the ceiling of the palace. He switched it on. How lovely the palace of bricks looked with the light shining inside!

The curly-haired doll found the bit of biscuit and put it on a tiny plate on the table. Meanwhile Panda and the toy dog carried the sweet bottle out of the toy shop and arranged the sweets on the table too. Just then there was a shout from Clockwork Mouse. He had found half a cup of lemonade that the children had left. It would make a fine drink for the King and Queen.

Then the teddy bear hid the musical box behind the coal scuttle. He began to turn the handle! The music sounded so lovely – everything was ready!

Just then, out from a hole in the floor boards came the King and Queen of the Mice! They had tiny crowns on their heads, and looked rather funny – but, dear me, they were the King and Queen all right! Twenty small mice followed them, blowing on twenty golden trumpets as they came.

The clockwork mouse, with a new blue bow round his neck, ran to welcome them all. Then he proudly lead them to the palace of bricks, bowing politely. The King and Queen were amazed and delighted.

"What a fine place you have here, Clockwork Mouse!" said the King. "And what lovely music!" said the Queen, looking all round for the band. But of course she didn't see the teddy bear hiding behind the coal scuttle, turning the musical box handle as fast as he could!

"And you've provided a feast too!" said the King, beginning to nibble the biscuit. "Very nice, Clockwork Mouse, very nice indeed."

"Look at these lovely sweets!" said the Queen Mouse, tasting one. "This surely must be one of the nicest places we have ever visited. It is most kind of you, little mouse."

After they had eaten, the King and Queen had a fine dance all around the palace and invited the toys to join in. Soon the whole nursery was filled with dancing figures and the poor teddy bear played the musical box till his arm nearly fell off.

In the middle of it all Jack and Tilly heard the musical box playing and came to see what was going on! How they stared when they saw what was going on!

Their palace of bricks shone like gold in the light of the toy lantern. And all over the nursery floor there were toys and mice playing and dancing to the sound of sweet music.

But as soon as the toys saw the two children they scampered inside the palace and hid, and Jack and Tilly thought they must have imagined the whole thing.

Anyway, the first light of morning was beginning to shine through the nursery window. It was time for the King and Queen to leave for Mouseland.

"Goodbye, Clockwork Mouse! Goodbye, toys!" they squeaked, as they disappeared through the hole in the floorboards. "We'll send you an invitation to our palace one day!" they said and the next minute they had gone.

Later that morning the children came to play in the nursery. The palace of bricks looked quite ordinary in the daylight and Jack and Tilly were disappointed to think that what they had seen had been nothing but a dream.

But can you guess what happened? Why, the toys had forgotten to take out the chairs and tables and lanterns.

"Goodness me!" exclaimed Jack. "So we did see something after all!"

"We wanted someone to live in our palace, and they did!" said Tilly, in delight.

As for the clockwork mouse, he is very happy now, for any day he is expecting an invitation from the King of the Mice to go and stay with him at *his* palace in Mouseland. I hope it comes soon, don't you?

2

Teddy and
the Elves

Illustrated by Kim Raymond

There was a new radio in the playroom. It had only just arrived, and the children were very excited about it. They had never had a radio before. "You just press this button here to turn it on," Emma explained to her little brother John. She pressed the round, red button on the front. There was a little "click" and, to the great astonishment of the toys who were listening, a band started to play. Teddy stared at the radio in surprise. The rag doll almost fell off the shelf, and the yellow cat was so frightened by the noise that she hid behind the blue dog.

The children were delighted with their radio. It had been given to them the day before by their Uncle John.

"May Emma and I keep it on, Mummy?" asked John.

"Yes – but not too loudly," said his Mother. "And make sure you keep it somewhere safe," she added. "I had a nice little radio that I kept on the shelf in the kitchen and it has completely disappeared. So has my best blue and white egg cup, *and* some of my silver spoons. You haven't seen them, have you children? I can't think where they can have gone."

But the children weren't listening to their mother. They were busy twiddling the knob on the front of the radio, instead, to see what different music they could find.

The toys thought the radio was wonderful. They listened to it all that day and all the next, and so did the children. They heard all sorts of different music and sometimes people even spoke out of the radio. The toys simply could not understand how they got in there. At other times, someone played the piano, and that seemed amazing too. How could a piano get inside such a small thing?

At night, when the children had gone to bed, the teddy bear looked longingly at the radio.

"It's magic," he said to the others. "It must be magic. How else can it have all those people inside it? I wish I could open it up and see exactly what is in there. How do you suppose you open it, Rag Doll?"

"Don't even *think* of such a thing!" cried the rag doll in horror. "You might break it."

"No I won't," said Teddy, and he began to undo a screw at the back. The rag doll had to get the big sailor doll to come and help stop him.

"We shall put you inside the brick box, if you don't solemnly promise to leave the radio alone from now on," said the rag doll. Teddy didn't want to be put into the brick box, so he had to promise.

But the next night Teddy wanted to press the red button that made the radio play. "I want to see the light come on, and hear the music play," he said. "*Please* let me press the button!"

"What! And wake up everyone in the house and have them rushing in here to see what's going on?" cried Rag Doll. "You must be mad." "But they wouldn't hear it," said the teddy bear. "Oh, do let me try. I promise to keep it quiet."

"You really are a very, very naughty teddy," said the rag doll. "You are *not* to press that button at all."

For the next two nights the teddy bear was quite good. But on the next night, he waited until the toys were playing quietly in the other corner of the room, then he crept over to the radio and pressed the button. The light shone inside and loud music began to play!

The toys were horrified! Clockwork Clown and Sailor Doll rushed over at once and pressed the button again. The light went out and the music stopped.

"Teddy! How naughty of you!" cried the sailor doll. "If you're not careful you will wake up the whole family. If they catch us, we will never be able to come to life at night again!" But Teddy didn't care. "They wouldn't have heard it," said Teddy. "It is you, with your big shouting voice, that will wake everyone up!"

And he ran off into the corner, squeezed himself under the children's piano, and refused to come out.

After that, Teddy wouldn't speak to any of the others, not even the little clockwork mouse who loved to chatter to him. It was very sad. Soon nobody asked him to join in the games, and the teddy bear began to feel very lonely indeed.

Deep down, Teddy knew that he should apologise to the sailor doll, and to all the other toys. But he was a proud teddy bear and he could not bring himself to say sorry.

Then one night, when the moon shone brightly outside the playroom window, Teddy could stand it no longer. He tried to join in with a game that the toys were playing, but they just ignored him.

Teddy was very upset. He walked away.

"Very well!" he called, over his shoulder. "If you won't play with me I'm going to find somewhere else to live!"

Out of the playroom door he went. The toys stared after him in horror. No toy ever went out of the playroom at night. Whatever was Teddy thinking of?

The moon shone brightly, and the teddy bear could see quite plainly where he was going. He went down the stairs, jumping them one at a time. They seemed very steep! He reached the bottom and looked round. Emma had sometimes taken him downstairs. He knew there was a room called the kitchen that had a nice smell in it. Which way was it?

Teddy found the kitchen door and squeezed round it. He was just about to cross the room when a shadow fell across the moonlit floor.

Teddy looked up in surprise. Had the moon gone behind a cloud?

No, it hadn't. It was somebody on the window-sill, blocking out the moon – and that somebody was climbing in the kitchen window! The teddy bear stared in surprise. Who could it be, coming in through the kitchen window in the middle of the night?

"It must be a robber!" thought Teddy in dismay. "They come in the night sometimes, and steal things. Oh, whatever shall I do? The toys will be even more cross with me if I make a noise and wake everyone up. Oh dear, oh dear, oh dear!"

Meanwhile, do you know who it was climbing in through the window?

Why, it was three naughty little elves.
They sprang quietly to the floor,
and were busy trying to open
the larder door.

Usually, they only came
to the kitchen looking for
bits of food – a slice of
currant cake, perhaps,
or some biscuits. But
sometimes, when they
were feeling very
naughty, they took
other things too.

Only the week before they had taken some things from one of the kitchen shelves and hidden them in the garden, but tonight they had only come to look for things to eat. Teddy watched as they started to fill their little knapsacks with food – sticky buns, pieces of cheese, and even some of Emma's favourite sweets.

Then one of the elves jumped up onto a shelf and started to pick up all sorts of other things for his sack – paper clips, a little key, a coloured crayon. Then he held something up that sparkled in the moonlight.

"Hello!" he said. "Look what I've found!" Teddy was dismayed to see that the elf was holding a beautiful ring which he quickly put into his sack.

"It must belong to Emma's mother," thought Teddy to himself. "She will be so sad to lose it."

And right there and then he decided that something must be done. So while the elves were still busy filling their sacks, Teddy slipped out of the kitchen and hurried upstairs as fast as he could go.

When he reached the playroom, he rushed through the door, panting. The toys looked at him in amazement.

"What's the matter? You look quite pale!" said the panda.

"Quick! Quick! There are three elves downstairs taking things from the kitchen!" cried the teddy. "We must stop them. Let's wake the humans up! Come on, make a noise everyone!"

All at once the toys started shouting. The panda growled as loudly as he could. The jack-in-the-box jumped up and down and banged his box on the floor. The toy mouse squeaked. But it was no good. No one could hear them.

No one woke up. Not a sound could be heard.

And then Teddy did a most peculiar thing! He gave a little cry, and rushed over to the radio. Before the toys could stop him, he pressed the little red button – and then he turned one of the knobs right round as far as it would go! The light went on inside the radio and a tremendous noise came blaring forth!

It was a man's voice, telling the midnight news; but the teddy bear had put the radio on so loudly that it was as if the man was shouting at the top of his voice.

"This will wake them up!" said Teddy.

And so it did! It also frightened
the elves in the kitchen so much
that they dropped the contents
of their knapsacks all over
the floor and made a
terrible noise trying
to scramble out of
the window.

But by the time
Emma's father had got to the
kitchen, they had quite gone.

"Must be those mice again!" sighed Emma's father, staring at the mess on the floor. Then something shiny caught his eye and he was surprised to find a ring lying amongst the crumbs...

Upstairs in the playroom, Emma and John were turning off the radio.

"This is what woke us up, Daddy," said John when his father appeared. "The playroom radio. But who could have put it on?"

Nobody knew. But Emma caught a gleam in Teddy's eye as he sat by the toy cupboard. Could *he* possibly have turned on the radio? Emma knew quite well she had put him back into the toy cupboard that evening – and there he was, sitting outside it! If she hadn't been old enough to know that toys can't walk and talk, she would have felt sure he had been up to something!

"The elves have gone! They won't come back after that fright!" cried the toys once everyone had gone back to bed. "Good old Teddy! *What* a noise the radio made, didn't it?"

Teddy was delighted to find himself such a hero. He beamed all over his face.

"Perhaps we can all be friends again now," he said hopefully.

"Oh, yes let's!" cried all the toys together. "It's so much nicer."

"And perhaps every so often you'll let me turn the radio on at night *ever* so quietly," added Teddy smiling.

"All right," said the sailor doll. "You deserve a reward, Teddy. You really were very clever."

Everyone agreed. And now when he feels like listening to a little music, the teddy bear turns the radio knob – very gently – and the music comes whispering out. Emma and John *will* be surprised if they hear it, won't they?

3

The Wishing
Carpet

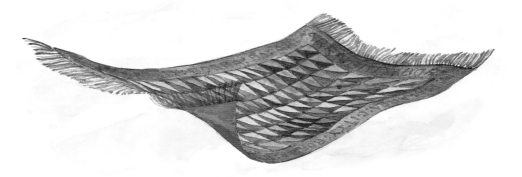

Illustrated by Pamela Venus

Once upon a time there were two children who owned a wishing carpet. A little old woman had given it to them in exchange for a basket of flowers. They had met her on Breezy Hill, and she had begged them to give her their basketful.

"Here you are, my dears," she said, when they handed her their flowers. "Here is something in exchange for your flowers. It is a magic carpet. Take great care of it."

They took it home and unrolled it. It was bright blue and yellow, with a magic word written in green round the border. Peter and Sally looked at the carpet in wonder.

"Gosh!" said Peter. "Suppose it really *is* magic!

Sally! Shall we sit on it and wish ourselves somewhere else and see what happens?"

"Yes," said Sally. So they sat themselves down and Peter wished.

"Take us to London," he said. The carpet didn't move. Peter spoke again.

"I said take us to London," he said, more loudly. Still the carpet didn't move. No matter what the two children did or said it just lay still on the floor and behaved like any ordinary carpet.

"It isn't a wishing carpet, after all!" said Sally, disappointed. "That old woman wasn't telling us the truth."

"What a shame!" said Peter.

So they rolled the carpet up and put it right at the back of the toy cupboard. They forgot all about it until about four weeks later when they met a very strange-looking little man in their garden.

"What are you doing here?" demanded Peter.

"Sh!" said the little man. "I'm a gnome. I've come to speak to you about your magic carpet."

"It isn't a magic carpet," said Peter. "It won't take us anywhere."

"Show the carpet to me and I'll tell you how to make it take you wherever you want to go!" said the gnome eagerly.

"Come on, then," said Peter, and he led the way indoors. But on the way Sally pulled at his sleeve.

"I don't like that little gnome at all," she said. "I'm sure he is a bad gnome, Peter. I don't think we should show him the carpet. He might want to steal it."

"Don't worry," said Peter. "I shall have a tight hold of it all the time!"

He pulled the carpet out of the toy cupboard, laid it on the floor and then sat on it. The gnome clapped his hands in joy when he saw it and sat down too.

"Come on, Sally," said Peter. "Come and sit down. This is going to be an adventure. Oh look, here's Scamp. He wants to come as well!"

So Sally and Scamp, the puppy, sat down beside the gnome and Peter.

"Did you say the magic word?" asked the gnome.

"Oh, no!" said Peter. "I didn't know I had to."

"Well, no wonder the carpet wouldn't move then!" said the gnome. "Listen!"

The gnome looked closely at the word round the border, and then clapped his hands twice.

"Arra-gitty-borra-ba!" he said. "Take us to Fairyland!" The carpet started to tremble and then rose in to the air.

The children gasped in
astonishment and held
on tightly as the carpet
flew out of the window
and headed west.

"Oh!" said Peter. "What an adventure! Are we really going to Fairyland?"

"Yes," said the gnome. "Watch out for the towers and pinnacles on its border."

Sure enough, before long the children saw shimmering towers and tall pinnacles on the blue horizon. The carpet flew on, and the world below seemed to flow away from them like a river.

"Fairyland!" cried Sally. "How lovely!"

They soon passed over a high wall, and the carpet flew downwards to a big market square. Then something dreadful happened! The carpet had hardly reached the ground when the gnome pushed Peter and Scamp off. But Sally was still on it with the gnome.

"Ha ha!" cried the gnome. "Now I've got Sally! She will be my servant and I've got the carpet for myself, foolish boy! Arra-gitty-borra-ba! Take me to my castle, carpet!"

Before Peter or Scamp could react, the carpet was flying high above the chimney tops. Peter groaned in despair.

"Oh dear, oh dear, whatever shall I do? I should have listened to Sally. Now that gnome will make her his servant and perhaps I'll never see her again!"

Scamp put his nose into Peter's hand, and to the boy's surprise, the puppy spoke.

"Don't worry, Peter," he said. "We'll get her back again."

"You can speak!" cried Peter in surprise.

"All animals in Fairyland can talk," said Scamp.

Peter looked round the market square. He saw many pixies, elves and brownies. They had seen what happened and came up to speak to Peter.

"Please help me," he said. "A horrid gnome took my sister away on a magic carpet. I don't know where they've gone, but I must get Sally back. She will be so frightened without me."

"That must have been Wily! He lives in a castle far away from here. Nobody dares to go near him because he is so powerful."

"Well, I *must* go and find him," said Peter bravely. "I've got to rescue my sister. Please tell me how to get to Wily's castle."

"The Blue Bird will take you to the land where he lives," said a pixie. "There you will find an old lady in a yellow cottage. She will tell you which way to go next."

Then one of the little folk took a silver whistle from his pocket, and blew seven blasts. In a few moments the sound of flapping wings was heard and a great blue bird soared over the market place. It flew down and the little folk ran to it.

"Blue Bird, we want your help," they cried. "Will you take Peter to the Land of Higgledy? His sister has been carried off by Wily the Gnome and he wants to rescue her."

"Certainly," said the bird. "Jump on."

So Peter and Scamp climbed
up on the Blue Bird's soft,
feathery back. He spread
his wide wings, and flew
off into the air. Peter
held tight, and Scamp
whined, for he was
rather frightened.

After flying for
half an hour, the
Blue Bird turned
his head round
and spoke to
Peter.

"We're nearly there," he said. "Can
you see some of the houses?"
Peter looked down. He saw a very
curious land. All the trees and houses
were higgledy-piggledy. The trees
grew twisted, and houses were
built in crooked rows. Their
windows and chimneys were
all lopsided.

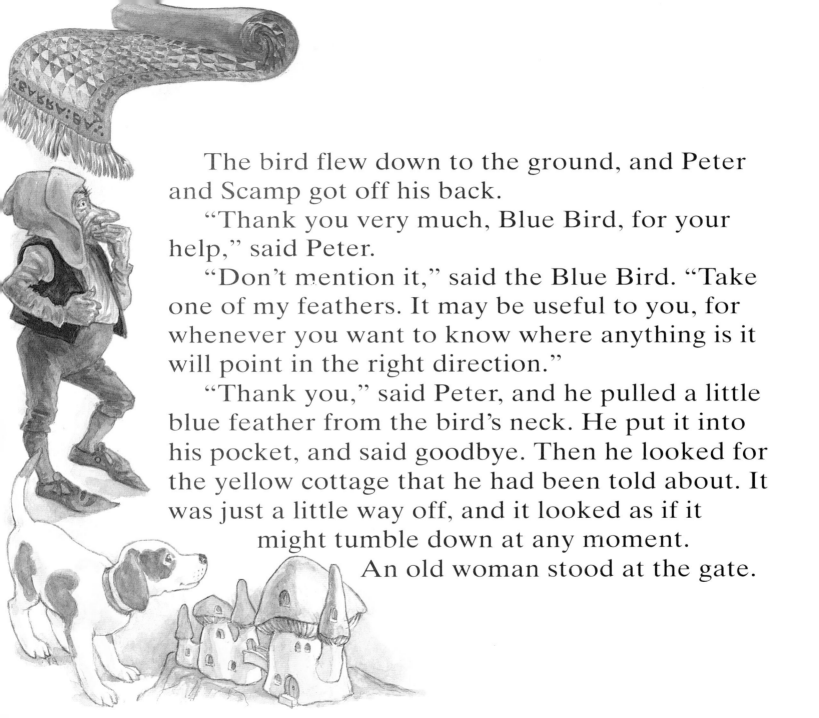

The bird flew down to the ground, and Peter and Scamp got off his back.

"Thank you very much, Blue Bird, for your help," said Peter.

"Don't mention it," said the Blue Bird. "Take one of my feathers. It may be useful to you, for whenever you want to know where anything is it will point in the right direction."

"Thank you," said Peter, and he pulled a little blue feather from the bird's neck. He put it into his pocket, and said goodbye. Then he looked for the yellow cottage that he had been told about. It was just a little way off, and it looked as if it might tumble down at any moment.

An old woman stood at the gate.

"Please," said Peter politely to the old woman, "could you tell me the way to the castle of Wily the Gnome?"

"I wouldn't go there," said the old lady. "That gnome is very wicked."

"I know," said Peter. "But he's got my sister, so I *must* find him."

"Dear, dear, is that so?" said the old woman. "Well, you must catch the bus at the end of the lane, and ask for Cuckoo Corner. Get off there, and look for a green flower behind the hedge. Sit on it and wish yourself underground. As soon as you find yourself in the earth, call for Mr. Mole. He will tell you what to do next."

"Thank you," said Peter.

Hearing the rumbling sound of a bus, Peter ran up the lane. At the top he saw a wooden bus pulled by rabbits. He climbed in and sat down with Scamp at his feet. The bus conductor, a duck, asked Peter where he wanted to go.

"Cuckoo Corner," said Peter. "How much is that, please?"

"We don't charge anything on this bus," said the duck, giving Peter a ticket as large as a post card. "I'll tell you when we get there."

Peter didn't need to be told when they had got to Cuckoo Corner because there was a most tremendous noise of cuckoos cuckooing for all they were worth! Peter hopped off the bus, and soon found the green flower.

"I've never seen a green flower before," he said to Scamp. "Come on, boy. Jump on my knee, or you may get left behind!"

He sat down on the flower and wished himself underground. Scamp gave a bark of fright as he felt himself sinking downwards, and Peter lost all his breath. They came to rest in a cave lit by glow-worms. Peter jumped off the flower.

"Mister Mole!" he shouted.
"Mister Mole! Where are you?"
Suddenly a door opened in the
wall of the cave and a mole with
spectacles on his nose appeared.

"Here I am," he said. "What do you want?"

"Please will you help me?" said Peter. "I want to rescue my sister from Wily the Gnome and I don't know what to do next."

"Well, this door leads to the cellars of Wily's castle," said the mole. "Come with me."

Peter followed the mole through the door into a large cellar. The mole led him to some steps.

"If you go up there you'll come to the gnome's kitchen," he said. "Go quietly, someone's there."

Peter listened, and sure enough he heard someone walking about overhead. He felt rather frightened. Suppose it was the gnome?

Peter crept very quietly up the steps – but then, Scamp suddenly whined and darted off.

He disappeared through a door at the top, and
Peter was left alone.

    Quietly Peter climbed the rest of the steps.
He thought that he could
hear someone crying.
He popped his head
round the door – and
there was Sally crying
and laughing over
Scamp.

    "Sally!" cried
Peter, and he ran
to hug her. How
pleased she was
to see him.

"That horrid gnome brought me to his castle and locked me in this kitchen," said Sally. "He says I'm to scrub the floor and cook his dinner. Oh, Peter, how can we escape from here?"

"I'll find a way!" said Peter, bravely – but just as he said that, his heart sank almost into his boots, for who should come stamping into the kitchen but the wicked gnome himself!

"Ha!" he said in surprise, when he saw Peter. "So you think you'll rescue your sister, do you? Well, you're wrong. There are no doors to this castle, and only one window right at the very top! You can't get out of there! Now I shall have two servants instead of one! You can start work by scrubbing the kitchen floor."

Peter watched in dismay as the gnome locked the cellar door with a large key. Sally began to cry.

"Don't be frightened," said Peter.

"There must be a way out!" He searched everywhere but there wasn't a single door that led outside, and not a window to be seen.

The gnome came into the kitchen again. He flew into a rage.

"Set to work!" he cried. "Fry me some bacon and eggs and make me some tea and toast." He stamped out of the kitchen. All three set to work, and soon the gnome's meal was ready on a tray. Peter carried it up to a tiny room. The gnome told him to put the tray down, and Peter ran back to Sally.

"If we're going to escape, we'd better do it now!" he said. "The gnome is busy eating. If only we knew where the magic carpet was!"

"What about that feather the Blue Bird gave you, Peter?" cried Scamp. "Can't you use that to find the carpet?"

"Of course!" cried Peter. He held the feather up.

"Point to where the magic carpet is!" he commanded.

At once the feather twisted round
and pointed towards the door that led
into the hall.

"Come on," cried Peter. "It will show us the
way!" They all went into the hall. Then the
feather pointed to the stairs. So they crept upstairs.

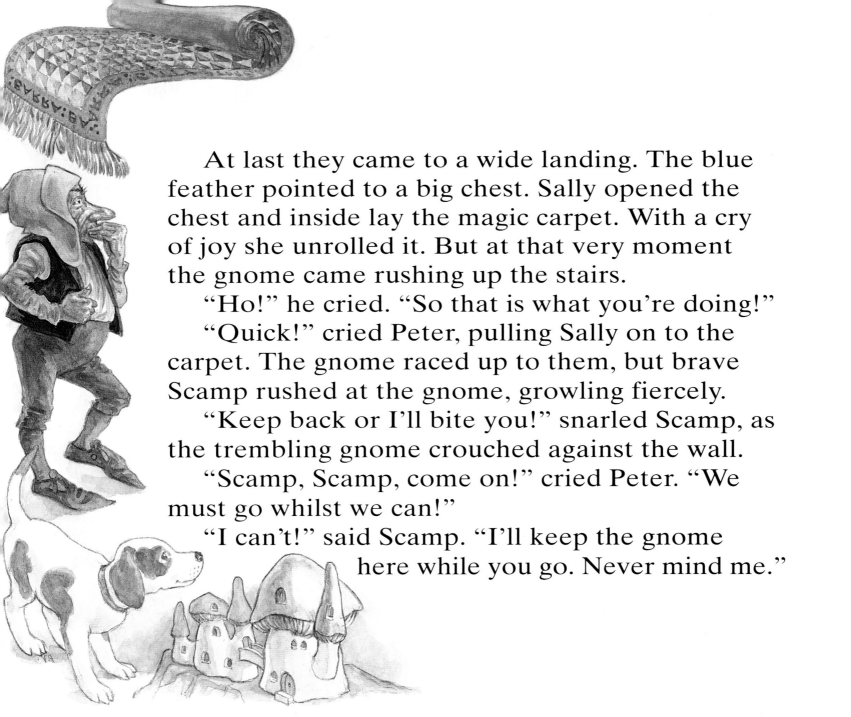

At last they came to a wide landing. The blue feather pointed to a big chest. Sally opened the chest and inside lay the magic carpet. With a cry of joy she unrolled it. But at that very moment the gnome came rushing up the stairs.

"Ho!" he cried. "So that is what you're doing!"

"Quick!" cried Peter, pulling Sally on to the carpet. The gnome raced up to them, but brave Scamp rushed at the gnome, growling fiercely.

"Keep back or I'll bite you!" snarled Scamp, as the trembling gnome crouched against the wall.

"Scamp, Scamp, come on!" cried Peter. "We must go whilst we can!"

"I can't!" said Scamp. "I'll keep the gnome here while you go. Never mind me."

Peter was sad to leave brave Scamp behind –
but he knew that he must rescue Sally.

"Arra-gitty-borra-ba! Take us home!" he cried.

At once the carpet rose from the ground and
flew upwards. It went up staircase after staircase,
until it came to a big open window right at the
very top. Just then Peter heard Scamp barking.

"Wait, wait!" he said to the carpet. But it
didn't wait. It flew out of the window and began
to sail away to the east. Peter was in despair.

Scamp appeared at the window . He saw the
carpet flying away, and he jumped. It was an
enormous jump, and he nearly missed the carpet!
He wouldn't have landed safely if Peter hadn't
caught his tail and pulled him on.

How happy they were to be going home together! Very soon they were over their own garden, and the carpet flew down to their nursery window. They all jumped off, and danced round in delight.

"Scamp, can you still talk?" asked Sally. "Wuff, wuff!" barked Scamp.

"Never mind," said Peter. "We understand your barks. What shall we do with the magic carpet?"

"Let's send it away in the air by itself!" said Sally. "*We* shan't want to use it again after all our adventures, I'm sure."

"All right," said Peter. He spoke to the carpet.

"Arra-gitty-borra-ba!" he said. "Rise up and fly round and round the world!"

At once the carpet rose and flew out of the window. It was soon out of sight. And, if you look carefully into the sky on a clear night, sometimes – just sometimes – you can see the wishing carpet still flying round the world.

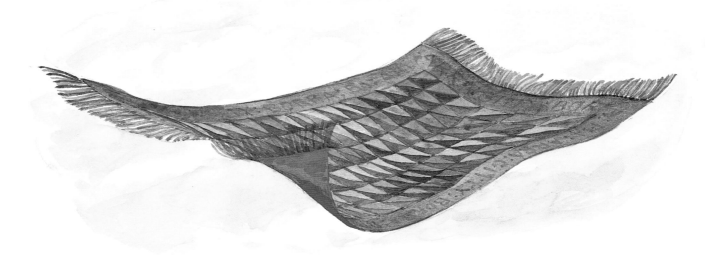